Evan's Extraordinary Friends

WRITTEN BY KANE L JONES

ILLUSTRATED BY DAN HARRIS

BEAR W!TH US PRODUCTIONS

-MEET THE GANG-

This is a story about Evan and his gang of extraordinary friends. Evan is a very special little boy because he has something called Down Syndrome. It isn't anything to be afraid of, it just means that Evan learns things a little slower than other boys and girls do.

Evan is a very funny little boy and can make anyone laugh. He has lots of friends, too many to count; but he has three very special friends, and their names are Dexter, Molly, and Penny. Evan and his three best friends go on all types of adventures and all have a lot of fun, which you are going to hear all about.

Each of them are very special and a little different in their own way. This makes them quite unique, and that's a good thing!

Let's find out a little more about all of Evan's extraordinary friends...

First there's Dexter, but his friends all call him Dex, he thinks it's cooler. Dexter loves to zoom around in his wheelchair, speeding past people and going super fast, "Turbo Dex coming through!!!" he often shouts. He needs his wheelchair because he can't use his legs as good as other people, and sometimes finds things like walking a little difficult. This doesn't matter to Dexter because it means he gets to be 'Turbo Dex' a lot more often.

Next there's Molly... she has always wanted to be a princess and has lots of pretty dresses which she loves to dress up in.

Molly pretends she's the prettiest princess in all the land. Molly is also very silly and sometimes even tries on her big sisters make up, only to be told by her big sister to take it off straight away. This makes Molly sad. Molly always enjoys cheering herself and the gang up with all the silly things she does.

The other girl in the group is Penny... Penny is very smart and always seems to know what the gang should do. If they are stuck or have a problem, the gang like to call her 'Problem Solver Penny'. Something Penny can do is talk with her hands. It's called sign language, and Penny can say all kinds of things by making different signs with her hands. Each sign means a different word.

Penny sometimes uses this because she's hearing impaired. That just means her little ears don't work very well and sometimes she can't hear the things that everyone else can; so now and again the gang have to speak louder to her. The good thing about being hearing impaired is Penny also gets to wear a really cool gadget on her ears that makes everything clearer. This gadget is called a hearing aid and Penny's is a bright glittery pink one.

So now you have met Evan's three best friends. These friends are who Evan gets up to all his mischief with. They are all very different in their own little way. If in some way you're like Evan, or one of his extraordinary friends, remember it's good to be different!

One day, Evan invited the gang to come and check out his new treehouse to see what mischief and fun they could all get up to. Penny and Molly wasted no time and rushed up the ladder to look inside the treehouse. When they got to the top, they saw for themselves that Evan's treehouse was the coolest thing ever, but something or someone was missing. Both girl's noticed 'Turbo Dex' was nowhere to be seen; that was because Dex was still outside in the garden and sadly he couldn't climb the ladder in his wheelchair.

The girls looked worryingly at Evan. They wondered how 'Turbo Dex' could get up into the treehouse with his chair. Evan smiled and reached over to a piece of dangling rope and pulled it hard... CRASH!!!, a ramp dropped to the ground and 'Turbo Dex' zoomed up into the treehouse as quick as a flash.

"See, said the two girls smiling, we didn't forget about y[...] 'Turbo Dex', there's always a way."

The gang were now all together in Evan's cool new treehouse; laughing and being mischievous as always and together they all got busy planning their adventures for the days to come.

—THE TREASURE HUNT—

One morning, Evan woke from his sleep to find it was a beautiful sunny day outside.

He remembered talking to the gang about visiting the beach and today seemed to be the perfect day to do it. They all met at the treehouse bright and early and with a big cheer, Evan and his very special friends excitedly headed out for some beach fun.

It was a lovely day at the beach. The sun was out and shining brightly in the sky and the gang were having an absolute blast, playing together on the sandy beach. They built sandcastles and wrote their names in the sand...
Penny and Molly both loved the beach and Evan did too.

They were all having the best day ever, apart from one of the gang. 'Turbo Dex' looked like he wasn't having very much fun at all. Evan wanted to cheer Dex up and asked him "What's wrong?"

Dexter it seemed, had simply just become bored of the sandcastles and now wanted the gang to play a game or do something more awesome and fun instead. 'Problem Solver Penny' had a brilliant idea, she thought the gang could all try and find some of the really cool stuff that might be hidden around the beach.

Silly Molly said, "I'm going to go and find myself a princess castle." She always keeps her friends smiling being silly like that, but you never know what you could find down on the beach.
'Turbo Dex' zoomed off in his wheelchair to search for hidden stuff. The wheels spun so fast, sand was flying all over the place. It was so much fun looking for things to find.

Before anyone else even had the chance to find anything exciting, Dexter shouted to come and see what he had found. With excitement, the gang rushed to Dexter to find him holding an old torn up treasure map.

"Is this what I think is?" asked Dex. Penny took a closer look at the map. Marked on it was a big X and Penny shouted with a cheer, "It's a treasure map and X marks the spot". Dexter and Molly excitedly looked at each other but Evan seemed slightly confused. Being a great friend, Penny explained to Evan, that 'X' marks the place on the map where the gang might find some buried treasure!

With great excitement, Evan and his extraordinary friends started the hunt for the hidden treasure. They all followed Penny, first passing some rock pools, then over an old washed up boat. All of a sudden, 'Turbo Dex' got his wheels stuck in some wet sand. The others tried to push and pull as hard as they could to free Dex but he was stuck fast. Then, with a big pull, 'Turbo Dex' was free from the sandy trap. "Yay", they all shouted and with that, they decided to go on with their adventure. Soon enough they reached a big, scary looking wooden cabin.

Penny looked at the map. It told her that the 'X' they had been searching for was inside that very cabin. The gang headed over to look for the hidden treasure but suddenly they all came to a halt.

Penny looked at Evan, he looked a little frightened. From inside the cabin, they could hear loud noises. First a loud BANG, then a huge CRASH!!!

As quick as they could, they all decided to hide.

Dexter and Evan both hid on one side of the cabin and Molly and Penny hid together on the other side. The gang all ducked down for cover. They desperately needed to speak to each other but how could they? They were on opposite sides of the cabin and they were too scared to shout.

'Turbo Dex' thought for a moment. He quickly realised that Evan could use the sign language that Penny had taught him. It was a great way to talk to her without making any noise. "Brilliant idea Dex," whispered Evan. He did his best to make the correct sign asking Penny what they should do next. With a knowing smile, Penny signed back. Of course, Extraordinary Evan understood the sign language perfectly and quickly realised the plan that was being hatched.

Using this special language, Penny had told Evan to look through the window to see what is inside. Evan and Dex quietly and carefully took a peek. Inside, the cabin looked quiet and they couldn't see anything in there at all.

They rushed inside the cabin for a better look, only to find that the cabin was empty and any possible treasure was nowhere to be found. They were all pretty disappointed, especially Molly, who now looked very sad indeed. Evan didn't like it that his friend was upset. "Don't be sad Molly, at least we had some fun searching. I'm sure we'll find treasure around here somewhere" he told her.

Dex looked at his friends, now all happy and smiling again, and said,

"I think we've already found treasure. We have the best and most special gang of friends ever".

Dexter was right, they were the best of friends. They all smiled, laughed and quickly got out of the cabin just in case whatever had made those loud noises came back. Then, off they went to enjoy what was left of their day at the beach.

—DAY OF PRETEND—

Evan and his extraordinary friends were all playing outside. They had already played all of their favourite games and were now getting a little bored; so now, they desperately needed a new one to play.

Evan scratched his head and thought really hard. What could they play?...

A great idea popped into Evan's head, the gang could use their imagination and have a day of pretend because using your imagination is great fun. Evan told the gang it would be perfect for a new game and they all agreed it would be fun and that it was exactly what they would do.

Molly, Penny and 'Turbo Dex' all liked the sound of that and so they all wondered what exactly they could play using their imagination. "Let's all be heroes for the day" shouted Evan. We can use our imaginations to help anyone in need. We can have cool hero names and super costumes too". Penny tells Evan that it's a brilliant idea and the rest of the gang join in with the same enthusiasm. So, they all got together and started to think of what heroes they could be.

It didn't take Dexter long to think of his hero, after all he already has his own cool superhero name. "Obviously you can just call me 'Turbo Dex',"he exclaimed. "I can turn my wheelchair into a super speeding rocket car, going as fast as the speed of light to save all who's in danger".

Penny was pretty quick to think of her superhero name too, "Well you can just call me 'Problem Solver Penny'. It's up to me to find people with problems that need solving".

Next up to claim a superhero name was Molly. "Mystic Molly is my name. I can read minds and sense when anyone is in danger, or needs help".

The gang had their hero names decided, but Evan still wasn't sure who he wanted to be. Dex had the perfect idea and suggested Evan should be in charge because everyone knows a superhero gang needs a leader. Evan loved that idea and immediately took his role very seriously. "Ok my extraordinary gang of superheroes, off we go to save the day!".

"Evan in charge, Evan in charge!" Said Molly.

"What is it 'Mystic Molly'?" Replied Evan.

"I've found a lady who needs our help. She's lost her puppy, he's called Patch, and she seems very worried indeed".
Evan immediately took control of the situation.

"Ok 'Problem Solver Penny' you're up first, see what you can do."

"I'm on it Ev!" Replied Penny.

Remember, Penny is hearing impaired and so her little ears don't work very well. That just means her little eyes work even better; so 'Problem Solver Penny' looked high and low and far and wide, and it didn't take her long to spot little patch about to cross a very busy road. Mystic Molly sensed danger and with a worried look on her face, exclaimed.. "Oh no Ev, those cars are heading straight for Patch."

"Ok 'Turbo Dex', it's your turn. I need you and your rocket car to zoom super fast and catch that 'K-9' before anything bad happens."

'Turbo Dex' hit the super speed button on his car and sped off as fast as he could to Patch's rescue. He dodged all the cars and all the danger, saving Patch just in the nick of time. Patch's owner was so happy that the gang had saved her little dog and said, "Thank you all so much, you're all the best super special heroes ever." Later that day, the lady invited Evan and his friends around to her house for tea and cakes as a thank you from her and Patch for saving him on the busy road.

Evan is very proud of his extraordinary friends and they are very proud of him too. The gang all learned that using your imagination sometimes is all you need to have fun. They also learned that you can be anyone, or do anything you wish, if only you put your mind to it.

Plus, they loved being heroes for the day and having tea and cake for tea. I'm guessing it won't be the last time they have a day of pretend!

—DEXTER'S NEW WHEELS—

One day, Dexter was visiting his special doctor.

Dexter goes to see his special doctor regularly so he can make sure he is healthy and doing well with his wheelchair.

Dexter's doctor is called Dr. Donald. Dexter sometimes enjoys going to see Dr. Donald, but sometimes he also gets scared and nervous about going to see him. It's ok to sometimes feel nervous because a lot of people feel like that on occasion, but it's nothing to worry about. Dex always remembers that he's 'Turbo Dex' and he's not afraid of anything!

On this particular day, Dr. Donald greeted Dexter as he entered the examination room and asked if he was feeling nervous. Dexter smiled and told him no, he's 'Turbo Dex', so of course he wasn't nervous, not one little bit.

The doctor smiled and told Dexter that today he had a big surprise for him.
Dexter was very excited to see what Dr. Donald had for him, but what could it be?

Dr. Donald told Dexter that it was time for him to have a new wheelchair, and what was even more exciting was that Dex could maybe help design it himself.
Dex couldn't stop smiling at the thought of a brand new turbo styled wheelchair.

The Doctor showed him a big book full of various designs for his new wheelchair. Dexter's face lit up with joy. He stared at the book with a huge grin, trying to decide on the style he liked the most; but there was so much to choose from, 'Turbo Dex' just couldn't make up his mind. Dr. Donald could see Dex was finding it hard to decide, so he told him that he could design his own chair if he wished.

Dexter loved that idea very much and his head started to fill with super-cool ideas on how his new chair should look. When he got home, he met the gang and told them the awesome news about his new chair and even though his head was spinning with great ideas, he still couldn't decide on how the chair should look.

Problem solver Penny' jumped up and had an idea. "We should all design Dexter a new wheelchair individually on paper and then he can choose his favourite one!" Evan thought it was a great idea, and so they all grabbed a piece of paper and got to work on this exciting project together.

After some quick sketching, Evan proudly held up his paper first and showed everyone his chair.
The chair looked awesome. It had bright red paint with orange flames over the wheels. This was because 'Turbo Dex' zoomed about that fast, he almost set his wheels on fire. On hearing this, 'Turbo Dex' nodded his head and smiled from ear to ear.

Molly was finished next. Silly Molly had made her wheelchair bright pink with princess crowns all over it. This was far too girly for Dex but he laughed about it and that made Molly smile.

Last but not least was Penny's drawing. She held up her piece of paper and it was like looking into space. The wheelchair had stars and planets all over it. There were even a few shooting stars too. Penny said she drew it like that, because her friend Turbo Dex was, "Out of this world"

Dexter loved them all, even Molly's silly one with all the crowns on. The gang asked Dex if he had a favourite, and he replied with a resounding, yes!
Can you guess which one was the winner?

Dex held up Penny's paper with the drawing of the stars on the chair high in the air and said, "I think we have a winner gang. I think this drawing is out of this world too"

The next day, 'Turbo Dex' sent the new wheelchair design to Dr. Donald. Dex hoped that it wouldn't take long to make as he couldn't wait for his awesome new space chair to arrive. He was so excited about the thought of blasting off and zooming around in his new chair as fast a shooting star!

-THUNDER AND FRIGHTENING-

Molly woke up after a good night's sleep full of smiles and feeling very happy indeed. Today was her birthday and just like you should be on your birthday, she felt very excited.

As part of her day, Molly had invited the gang for an afternoon out at a funfair as a special birthday treat. When it was time, she excitedly made her way to meet her friends at the

entrance to the fairground. They all greeted her with cheers of "Happy Birthday Molly," and each member of the gang looked forward to the fun ahead.
Molly had put on her best dress and looked like a beautiful birthday princess.

Earlier that morning the sun had been shining but now it was afternoon and thick grey clouds were gathering overhead. It started to get quite dark and small drops of rain started to fall from the sky.

All of a sudden a storm hit and it started to rain very heavily indeed.

Luckily, Molly had also invited her extraordinary friends for a sleepover at her house later that evening, and so they quickly headed back to her house to get in from the rain.

"Sleepovers are so much fun" said Molly. This was Evan's first sleepover and he couldn't wait...

"What games can we play?...

"Where will I sleep?...

"What else do you do on sleepovers?" asked Evan, excitedly.

Evan was so excited he just couldn't calm down. It made Molly giggle quite a bit!

Evan was so excited about the sleepover that he forgot that the first thing to do was to sing happy birthday to Molly. So, as soon as he calmed down that's exactly what they did. They all sung to their best friend as she blew out the candles on her birthday cake.

Can you guess what kind of cake Molly had for her birthday?

That's right, just like the gang expected, it was a princess cake. Molly looked at the big birthday cake and said to the gang, "You are what you eat, so this makes me a pretty princess for real." They all laughed, "Silly Molly" they all said, and then they all tucked into a lovely piece of delicious birthday cake.

After the cake was eaten, the gang tried to think of what they can do next. It was still too wet to play outside, and so they all decide to play hide and seek indoors, which was one of their favourite games to play together.

Penny closed her eyes, and counted to ten. Evan, Molly and 'Turbo Dex' all hid from Penny in secret places around Molly's house. "Ready or not, here I come!!!" she shouted, and started searching for the well hidden gang.

The rain outside was now getting quite heavy and as the storm grew louder, Penny searched for her friends high and low throughout the house. The noise of the heavy rain bouncing loudly off the windows was making it hard for Penny's hearing aid to hear any of the noises the gang might have been making.

So to help Penny search, she used her other senses instead, she used her keen eyesight, and quickly caught a glimpse of something moving behind the cupboard door. She opened the door to find 'Turbo Dex' crouching down close to the floor. "One down, two to go" she said to herself.

Next, she used her nose and sniffed the air like a little dog to sense any unusual smells. Penny could smell Molly's birthday cake coming from under her bed. Who's under there I wonder, any ideas?... she thought to herself. She took a peek, only to find both Evan and Molly stuffing their faces with Molly's princess cake. They started to giggle and the cake sprayed out from their mouths.

Penny had found them all by using her other senses. She felt very proud indeed.

All of a sudden they all heard an extremely loud and scary clap of thunder. It was very loud and shook the house. Evan was frightened but Penny put her arms around him and told him it was ok and that there was nothing to be scared of. Evan and his gang of extraordinary friends were all safe and sound inside the house.

Evan immediately felt much better and looked around for Dex. He was nowhere to be seen. The group all decided that he must be hiding from the thunder and lightning because he didn't like it, and it scared him too.

They all searched for Dex and eventually found him hiding in the bathtub. They all gave him a hug and made sure he was ok.

"I thought 'Turbo Dex' wasn't afraid of anything" said Molly with a cheeky grin. Feeling a little sorry for them, Penny then told both Dex and Evan that it's ok to be frightened and that it's normal to be scared sometimes. In fact it happens to everybody, she explained. "Even grownups? asked Dex. "Yes, even grownups, replied Penny.

The next day when they all woke up, the rain had cleared and the sun was shining again; and a big beautiful rainbow covered the sky.

"See gang, sometimes something big and scary can always turn into something beautiful like this, you just have to get through the scary part first" Penny said. The gang all gazed up at the big beautiful rainbow and smiled.

-TRICK OR TREAT-

Tomorrow was halloween, and halloween was Evan's favourite time of year. Evan loved Halloween because he got to dress up and go out collecting lots of treats while 'trick or treating' with his extraordinary friends.

This year, Evan's school were having a costume contest, and the winning team would receive a gigantic bag of sweets and other treats as a prize. This was simply perfect for Evan and he began to think of what his winning costume could be.

Evan began to think of ideas for him and his friends straight away. Evan really wanted to win that gigantic bag of treats. 'Turbo Dex' was also thinking hard about what they could be, and asked his friends what they thought would make a great costume.

Evan had plenty of ideas to share, and Molly, Penny, and Dex couldn't wait to hear them.

With a big smile on his face, Evan told them that they could all be superheroes, pirates or maybe even something funnier?

Before Evan could even get his words out to tell his friends more of his ideas, Dexter chose his favourite and decided he loved the idea of being a superhero.

Evan and the gang would be brilliant superheroes, because they'd be the best super special heroes in the world.

So just like that, thanks to Dex, they all decided that being superheroes would be a winning combination and all got to work right away on their costumes.

The next day Molly had some bad news for everyone. Some of the gang's friends from school had also decided to go as superheroes too. They all couldn't wear the same kind of outfits as they wouldn't win anything. They were all very disappointed.

Evan really wanted that big bag of treats, so they put on their thinking caps, and 'Problem Solver Penny' stepped up with another great idea. "Well, she said, we're all different and special in our own ways, so instead of being all the same as each other dressed as superheroes , let's all be something different because remember, being different is good".

Well it seemed 'Problem Solver Penny' had once again saved the day. Evan and the gang liked the idea a lot. They didn't have much time so they had to think and act fast. They decided to meet up at the contest and to surprise each other with the costumes they had chosen, so off they went to quickly get ready.

First to arrive at the contest was 'Turbo Dex'. Dex has turned himself into an army soldier and his wheelchair had become a big green army tank. So far all eyes were on him. Next, Molly arrived and I'm sure you can guess what her costume was.

Yes, that's right, she turned up as the prettiest princess in all the land.

Evan decided to go as a pirate. He did look amazing with a fake beard, a pirate hat, and he even had a trusty parrot on his shoulder.

Last, but certainly not least, was Penny. Penny dressed up as an astronaut; she wore a cool space helmet. Her hearing aid was now an earpiece to talk to mission control, just like the real astronauts use in space to talk to everyone. The gang all loved each other's costumes and they really thought they could win. They nervously headed out onto the stage with everyone else to find out who was going to be taking home that perfect prize...

All of a sudden, a voice from a loudspeaker situated above the stage said...

"Due to their creativity and diversity, the winner of the costume contest is...

"Evan and his extraordinary friends!!!"...

The gang did it, they had won the first prize together as a group.

"See gang, it's always good to be different" said Penny.

They proudly took their prizes and off they went back to Evan's tree house to open their sweets and treats. They all sat together laughing and gave each other high fives in between stuffing sweets into their mouths. It was the best Halloween ever!!

THE END.

Evan's Extraordinary Friends

"DO NOT PASS JUDGMENT ON SOMETHING YOU DO NOT UNDERSTAND, SIMPLY OBSERVE AND LEARN"

WRITTEN BY KANE L JONES

BEAR WITH US PRODUCTIONS

Printed in Poland
by Amazon Fulfillment
Poland Sp. z o.o., Wrocław